Consultant, Istar Schwager, holds a Ph.D. in educational psychology
and a master's degree in early childhood education.
She has been an advisor, consultant, and content designer for numerous parenting,
child development, and early learning programs including the *Sesame Street*
television show and magazines.
She has been a consultant for several Fortune 500 companies
and has regularly published articles for parents
on a range of topics.

Louis Weber, C.E.O.
Publications International, Ltd.
7373 North Cicero Avenue
Lincolnwood, Illinois 60646

Permission is never granted
for commercial purposes.

Manufactured in the U.S.A.

8 7 6 5 4 3 2 1

ISBN 1-56173-480-2

active minds

my day

PHOTOGRAPHY
George Siede and Donna Preis

CONSULTANT
Istar Schwager, Ph.D.

Publications
International,
Ltd.

Good morning! It's time to
wake up and get dressed.

Pick out the play clothes
that you like the best.

Time for play with girls and boys.

Let's be friends and share our toys.

Lunch is over.
Who wants
to go out?

Off to the park!
Let's skip,
swing, and shout!

These toys are good
for quiet play

When you are tired
late in the day.

Dinner means many
   good things to eat.

Come to the table
   and take your seat.

Bath time is always
more fun than you think.

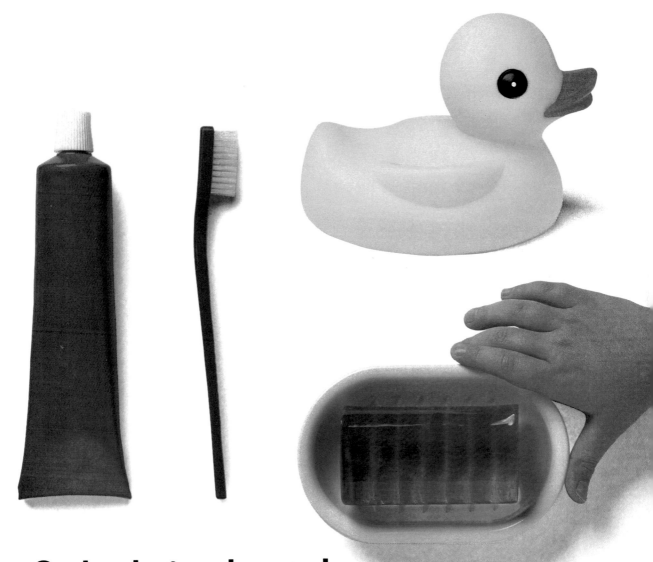

Splash in the tub,
brush your teeth at the sink.

Cuddle in bed now.
Get sleepy and snug.

Good night! Sleep tight!
Here's a kiss and a hug.